Rocky

THE CAT WHO BARKS

Donna Jo Napoli
AND
Marie Kane

ILLUSTRATED BY
Tamara Petrosino

Dutton Children's Books • New York

For our grandchildren
—D.J.N. & M.K.

To Ryan & Jill, with love
—T.P.

Text copyright © 2002 by Donna Jo Napoli and Marie Kane
Illustrations copyright © 2002 by Tamara Petrosino
All rights reserved.

CIP Data is available.

Published in the United States 2002 by Dutton Children's Books,
a division of Penguin Putnam Books for Young Readers
345 Hudson Street, New York, New York 10014
www.penguinputnam.com
Designed by Richard Amari
Printed in Hong Kong
First Edition
1 3 5 7 9 10 8 6 4 2
ISBN 0-525-46544-8

Rocky used to live in a small house with Old Nini.

Old Nini liked to sit in the bright sunlight. It warmed her bones and knobby fingers. Her eyes weren't so good, so the sunlight helped when she knitted.

Rocky sat at her feet. Now and then he chased yarn balls around the room.

But mostly he sat, happy and sassy.
Their life was quiet. The only noise around
the house was Rocky's bark.

Then Old Nini got even older, and she had
to move in with her son, who lived in an
apartment building that didn't allow dogs.
   Rocky had to move to the house with the
little monsters.

The little monsters made faces. The little monsters threw blocks. The little monsters shouted. When their pudgy hands came at him, Rocky ran.

But even worse were the five cats who lived
in the little monsters' house. They were

Misha, the big,
mean mother cat,

and Cappuccino, who had
such thick fur she looked
like a lamb,

and Crystal Kitty,
with the long hair,

and Cally, the only one who
was smaller than Rocky,

and Latte, with
blue, blue eyes.

When Rocky lived with Old Nini, no one told him what to do. In fact, he bossed Old Nini pretty good.

But when Rocky pranced up to these cats and barked, they arched their backs and hissed.

They circled him, showed their claws, and spat. Rocky whimpered and rolled onto his back.

The cats walked off, and Rocky slunk behind
the couch and hid with his special blankie that
Old Nini had knitted for him.

That was not all the cats did to Rocky.

Misha knocked him
aside and ate from his
dish, every last morsel.
Rocky had nothing to
gnaw on but hard dog
biscuits.

Rocky had a red
turtleneck sweater.
But Crystal Kitty
rolled on it and left
her fishy-smelling cat
hair everywhere.

Rocky had a very nice bed that he'd brought with him. But Latte gave him an icy stare, and then she took it.

Cally, the kitten, bit a hole in his rubber hamburger.

Cappuccino swatted his leash with her claws and shredded the end up bad.

Whenever Rocky let out even the smallest little bark, the cats glared at him. Rocky spent most of his time behind the couch, silent. All he had was the blankie that Old Nini had knitted.

On weekends, along with the cats, the little monsters were home all day.

The little monsters were loud. They knocked over furniture and roller-skated across the room. They squirted water guns and swung on the curtains.

The cats played together and paid no attention to the little monsters. But Rocky was scared. And he was sad, too. The cats had fun with each other. The little monsters had fun. But Rocky hadn't had fun in a long time.

One day the little monsters decided to play house. They put a pile of baby clothes in the center of the floor. One of them caught Cally, and the other one caught Misha.

One little monster put a dress on Cally. Then she tied a frilly bonnet under Cally's chin.

The other little monster put a jacket and big floppy booties on Misha.

When Misha tried to rip the booties off, one little monster grabbed her tight. Both of them ran and laughed and jumped on the couch, holding the cats.

Cally and Misha meowed loudly.
Rocky didn't know what to do. So he sat very still. He was scared.

The little monsters wrapped up Cally and
Misha in baby blankets. Then they opened a
backpack and prepared to stuff in the cats.

Crystal Kitty and Cappuccino and Latte
watched from the windowsill. Their eyes were
huge. Their tails twitched.
"Meowww," whined Cally and Misha together.
But the little monsters paid no attention.
Rocky stood up. He trembled all over.

He bounded across the room and barked louder than he ever had at Old Nini's place. The whole house rang with his bark.

The little monsters' mother came running. She scolded them and took the baby clothes off Cally and Misha.

Rocky went back behind the couch and curled up with his blankie.

The next day, the little monsters went to school. It was quiet in the room.

The cats were sitting here and there. But Rocky felt them all looking at him.

Latte walked slowly across the room and sat beside Rocky. She licked him. Something strange was happening. Rocky licked back.

Later Misha stood over her own dish instead of Rocky's. She swatted Rocky a hunk of cat food. It smelled fishy, but not so bad. Rocky ate it.

Then Crystal Kitty and Cappuccino tied
Rocky up in a ball of yarn. The yarn reminded
him of the good old times. Rocky liked it.

Cally lay in the sun, doing
nothing. Rocky lay down
beside her. It felt a little
bit like when he used to
sit in the warm sunlight
at Old Nini's feet.

That night, Rocky licked his paws and washed
his face, just like the cats. He yawned wide,
just like the cats.

Now every day Latte, Cally, Crystal Kitty, Cappuccino, Misha, and Rocky play together, eat together, and sleep together.

But Rocky is the only cat who barks.